Jama

Nov 2003

SMALL STREAMS OF LOVE AND HATE

Damon Kamming

MINERVA PRESS

LONDON
ATLANTA MONTREUX SYDNEY

SMALL STREAMS OF LOVE AND HATE
Copyright © Damon Kamming 1998

ISBN 0 75410 427 3

First Published 1998 by
MINERVA PRESS
Sixth Floor
Canberra House
315–317 Regent Street
London W1R 7YB

Printed in Great Britain for Minerva Press

SMALL STREAMS OF
LOVE AND HATE

This book is dedicated to the loving memory of Jeanie Gemmill (13/4/14–5/9/97).

Acknowledgements

Thanks to all my friends and enemies (you know who you are). Mum and Dad for all your love and support. Jodi and Asha for being such fucking cool sisters, not to mention my best friends. Amen.

'Without a family, man alone in the
world trembles with the cold.'

André Maurois
The Art of Living

Preface

A vitriolic diatribe against the grain. This tirade includes rhyming couplets of concern and sweet soliloquies of desire. *Small Streams of Love and Hate* is a sumptuous caustic catharsis from the heart.

'I detest that man who hides one thing in the depths of his heart and speaks forth another.'

Homer
Iliad

Contents

Part Three
Pathos

Part Four
Revenge

Part Five
Anger

Part Six
Self-Destruction

Part Seven
Recovery

Part Eight
Redemption

Part One

Lust

'Blood stains
Speed kills
Fast cars
Cheap thrills
Rich girls
Fine wine
I lost my sense
I lost control
I lost my mind.'

Agent Orange
Blood stains

Blade

Sifting
shifting great hulks of desire
from my head
my bed

through shrouds of temptation
desire
denial
force fed

frank blood on white sheets
sacred cow
holy grail
hail, hail

taken with a sharp intake of breath
forbidden fruit
cuts to the quick
stiletto flick drip, drip.

Rivulet

Sink into my sweet symphony
fall into my abyss
taste my blooded lips and take my breath away.

Couplets of Concern

She was a full blooded red wine
illuminating the room
intoxicating all in her company

he exuded the menace of darkness
creating swathes of unease
enjoying all the attention

nothing is more attractive than disinterest
like a switchblade across a cheek
his indifference made her smart

never was she more vivacious
drawing him into her spell
with a pout crimson red

stark in his desire
he was never more dangerous
together they burned

spellbound, others watched in awe
to see who would be destroyed
all consuming such was their fate.

Undulating Motion

Take me on a journey
eclipse my reality
facilitate the swaying motion of my soul.

Succulent Opulence

Inflamed blooded lips
cut in moments of passion
instil within my soul
the desire that burns

embers glowing in the dark
casting shadows over your body
illuminating the sheen of perspiration
over the grace of your form

intoxicated with your opulence
the throb of my heart
threatens to engulf me
when I take you between my lips
and devour all your senses.

Captivate Me

Dilate my pupils with awe
flush my face with desire
send shivers down my spine
electrocute my sense of reason
save me from myself
destroy me with your rapture.

Higher

If the devil is god's most beautiful creation
Then sin is his rapture
A fornicator and adulterer
Son of man or creature of god
Cast forth and behold your evil angels.

'Well here I come I'm on the run
Who wants to fight temptation. That's no fun.
C'mon and play the games don't you feel no shame
That's what Eve said to Adam before she came'.

Social Distortion
Pleasure Seeker

Part Two
Love

'I chased the heat of her blood
Like it was the holy grail
Descend beautiful spirit
Into the evening pale.
Her appaloosa's
Kickin in the corral smelling rain
There's a low thunder rolling
'Cross the mesquite plain.
But there's just dry lightning on the horizon line
It's just dry lightning and you on my mind.'

Bruce Springsteen
Dry Lightning

White Content

Sanctified by the spirit of you
crucified on a cross of blood red roses
justified by the smile painted inside my chest

her warmth melted his resolve
as a heater onto ice his hard edges smoothed out
where once there was a rock now rivers of dreams flow.

Pellegrino

As one man's heart contracts
another's relaxes
with my eyes open
I see yours shut.

Absolution

Undeniable yet so inexplicable
ask a man why he loves you so
and he is unable to
instead head bowed he smiles
at the wonder of it all.

Blue Note

Stricken by the depth of colour, sound and serenity
stricken into a state of calm
calmed by the intensity of it all.

Vitriol

He liked the sound of his own voice
she made him eat his words.

Zezette

She consumed his love
and died
empty and distraught
he lived.

Round the Corner

Happy and content
take heed

peer round the corners
with trepidation

grasp on to all you hold dear tightly
in a cruel second all may disappear

with nothing left
you will question everything.

'Already in spite of myself I had entered into your life so that one day in spite of myself I should remain thus at the portals of your death.'

Simone De Beauvoir
The Blood of Others

Part Three
Pathos

'Dear lover, I can't take the pain no more
Dear lover, I pick my heart up from the floor
Dear lover, I can't believe it's come to this
Dear lover, give me one last painful kiss.'

Social Distortion
Dear Lover

Depths of Despair

Barely gasping for breaths of sanity
choking on this suffocating depression
eyes perpetually brimming with tears
I swallow hard

nervously clutching at straws
dreaming of tranquil sunsets
my chest rose with hope
I dared to live

she came into my life
like the first rays of sunshine
after a lifelong winter
she left town on the arm of a more honourable suitor

painfully alone
me and my thoughts
together once again
I close my eyes and pray for sleep.

Empty Lovesick

Hollow sorrow
what for tomorrow?

Heartfelt concern
emotionally shorn

brooding unease
where is she?

melancholy longing
forever waiting

another night with yourself
alone at home on the shelf

gazing at the ceiling
what ifs become exquisitely appealing.

Shining Path

Pitifully scorned
without thought to reason

frequently adorned
in a halo of righteousness

secretly mourned
from the corners of my conscience.

Protection

Cover me with your obsession
my crescent of hope
the eclipse of my melancholy

protect me from the barrage
the slight of hands
the turn of heads

provide my *joie de vivre*
the *raison d'être*
failing that, my *coup de grâce*.

Being Alone

Without your crutch
not much.

Raison D'Être

Cascades of swollen broken dreams
flow where desire once thrived
melancholy and reflective

sitting questioning
face in my hands
heart on my sleeve.

Throes of Pathos

In a chasm
down where I abide

nuance and reflection
replaced by muscle spasm

agitated and irritated
knuckles white and blooded

I bear evidence
sensitised yet numbed

The crimes of humanity
gnawing at my soul.

'Now hatred is by far the longest pleasure
Men love in haste, but they detest at leisure.'

Lord Byron
Don Juan

Part Four

Revenge

'Hold out your hand to me
Give me your hand
I'll bite it off…

Black Flag
Damaged

Paucity

Inward, backward, downward
involution
confusion
submission

number all through the summer
negation
fertile imagination
masturbation

dimmer, colder, shorter
winter
fuck her
bit-her.

Lusting

Screaming
searing
searching

for somebody to devour

aching
arching
asking

for someone to take it

satiated
suffused
swollen

for some more.

Your Spare Change

Spare me your sympathy
and your second-hand philosophies

grant me my freedom
from all my indiscretions

chastise me for my honesty
when I cut off my nose
to spite my face.

Dispossessed

Sitting here
twitching
itching
gnashing my teeth
biding my time

so much shite trite
sickly sweet
makes me bilious
nauseous and tremulous

you don't know me
you really have no idea
how can you contemplate my failings
when I don't give a fuck about you or your feelings!

Spurned

With blistering fury
he sliced and slashed
in the process burned and spurned

he's all alone
staring at the gutter
and wondering how the hell he got there.

'I am
I'll be
I will
You'll see
I am
I'm me.'

Twisted Sister
I Am (I'm Me)

Part Five

Anger

'Shut your fucking mouth
I don't care what you say
You keep talking
Talking everyday
First you're telling stories
Then you're telling lies
When the fuck
Are you gonna realise
That I don't want to hear it?
Know you're full of shit.'

Minor Threat
I Don't Wanna Hear It

Fist in Your Face

My teeth grind
my head seethes
my, my
just one more thing
my friend.

Mirror, Mirror

Shattered tatters of life
shower me with your discontent
I will wear it on my face
your pain reflected
ugly isn't it?

Plenty of Time

Legions of troops march over my pains
trampled into the dirt

boots break my back
malice crushes my soul

teeth grinding I take the punishment
slowly I begin to enjoy it

rising from the dirt
twisted, blooded and mutilated

seeking revenge I start to need it
my pains, those fuck stains.

Dinner Party

Your talk of cookies and muffins
and so and so
and isn't he sweet
and mummy and daddy
and what's his name

your soft stupid mouths
sliced open and babbling your nonsense
that little wagging tongue
cut out
and stuck up your ass
so that you can taste the shit
I have to listen to every single day.

Abyss

Enshrouded in a blackness
darker than your worst fears
unable to open my mouth
for fear of uttering unspeakable truths

struggling to draw breath
to move in this overbearing shroud
hate and loathing fuel my day
dreaming of solace in pain.

'It feels good to say what I want
It feels good to knock things down
It feels good to see disgust in their eyes
I'm gonna go wild
Spray paint the walls.'

Black Flag
Spray Paint (The Walls)

Part Six

Self-Destruction

'And now I've the most charming of verandahs
I sit and watch the junkies, the drunks
And pimps and whores.
Five green bottles sitting on the floor
And I wish to Christ, I wish to Christ
That I had fifteen more.'

The Pogues
Boys From the County Hell

Dope

She is a bit much sometimes
and often not enough.

Shit

Everything is all just a bunch of shit
My arms look like the fucking Somme
I've been poppin and my muscles
They've been dripping pus.

I can't get it together
I can't you cunt
My mind is screaming
Screaming for some fucking relief.

'Chained to the needle and the spoon'
Ain't no fucking swaggering Britpop
Chorus because like Neil Young says,
'Every junky is like a setting sun.'

New York, New York

The lower east side
jitters and jives
and barely survives

gnashing and chattering
like a speed freak's jaws
it keeps me alive.

Delirium Tremens

Voices specified
visions identified
horrors realised

experiencing formication
agitation and desperation
humiliation instead of adulation

once a star
blazing in his own microcosmos
now in the throes of pathos

seeking absolution
pleading for redemption
suffering to the end in isolation.

Man in Motion

Propeller head
bucketbrain
have you no shame?
With every concession
and submission
and reconciliation
you sink deeper into hopeless humiliation.

Old Sod

The bastard flinched
aye, aye lament on
old jakey's fucking fiction

nailed his colours to the cross
and hung himself
skewed and draped down the wall

burst blooded bloated face
grinning and reeking
shitting his shambolic mortal coil

incontinent and belligerent
it's good for a man to let loose once in a while
so the bastard's father told his son.

'I want to live
I wish I was dead.'

Black Flag
What I See

Part Seven

Recovery

'The darker the night – the brighter the stars.
The deeper the grief – the closer is God.'

Fyodor Dostoyevsky
Crime and Punishment

A City Tale

The crisp clarity of an autumn morning
augmented by the aroma of freshly ground coffee

the city comes to life clear in mind
purposeful in its advance toward night
I sit and enjoy the liberating anonymity.

Sifting

When times are hard
shift down a gear
more traction for the slippery slopes ahead

if depression comes a calling
hold on, ride the storm
blues pass with the winds of change

should despair knock on your door
greet him, invite him in
then show him the error of his ways

face the bad times
with head held high
ride the punches

you'll bounce back
off the ropes
a stronger and better man.

Hardcore

Whenever I get soft
tired and dejected
full of self-doubt
fearful of the new
bitter and twisted
sick with hate
you are always there.

Straight Edged

I have so much respect for you all
pouring scorn over all the lies
speaking the truth
keeping it real

no need to find courage
in a bottle of beer
solace and hope
in a syringe of dope
happiness and joy
in a white tablet of hope

I crave a new dawn
straight edged crisp and clear
moving ahead
this is it can't you see?

Beaten Paths

Compromise and don't forget to choose
the middle ground
the high mountains of possibilities
obscured by the fear of failure
myopic meandering donkeys
kissing ass for the want of a raise

elevate your mind
clear the misgivings from your heart
otherwise like a clot in an artery
living tissue will die
then again fuck them
that's natural selection for you.

Had It

Seen it, been there, done that
bought the T-shirt
have you fuck
you blithering fools

grow up, be mature, act your age
not your shoe size
why?
And be all washed up like you?

Relax, mellow out, go with the flow
no way man
make a stand
be yourself, against the grain
don't succumb to the banal.

See Through You

Bullshit flies and hits me
full in the face
stings like shrapnel
bleed for these fools
never

shrug it off
wounds heal
scar tissue forms
strength for the next assault
watch out big fella.

Sell Out

Will you make a stand?
Will you stand tall?

Will you sell yourself short?
Will you sell your soul?

Will you be true to yourself?
Will you take a fall?

Will you?

When I outdo myself
When I do it to you

When I sell myself
When I sell you short

When I lie to myself
When I lie next to you.

'If you're gonna build a house
Make it a home.
If you're gonna pull some weight
Pull your own.
If you're gonna help
Reach out your hand.
If you're getting up
Then take a stand.'

Ben Harper
Fight For Your Mind

Part Eight
Redemption

'This for the books I never dared to write
This for the journeys I never made
This for everybody in general whom I
Wanted to hate and tried to understand.'

Jean-Paul Sartre
Iron In The Soul

One Chance

No compromise
spectacular and shocking
make a difference
as Thrasher says,
'The more you live, the less you die.'

You only get one shot
to put it off for another day
a gluttonous waste
as Henry says,
'Hero time… time to shine.'

Blueprint for Success

Fused my fucking brain
Split all my muscles
Spilled my guts

Trying to get ahead

Read Dale Carnegie
Smiled, listened, won friends
Influenced people

Trying to get ahead

Woke up
Looked in the mirror
Someone else looked back

Trying to get ahead.

A Balcony of Angels

Snowflakes
cool not cold
transform

hate
easy not hard
deform

love
righteous not wrong
forlorn.

Understand

Understand me that when I thank you
I do so from the bottom of my heart

understand also that when I hate you
I do so from the depths of my soul

understand finally that when I love you
I do so for ever.

Opus

Cinnamon-scented dusted chapel
hands laid bare the velvet-lined casket
enveloped his memory in silence

musk and the lingering of incense
mourned for her love lost tragedy
death and the futile grace of his demise.

Belief

As the stars pierce the darkness
and the rainbow through the rain
hope will transcend despair.

Memories

Cerebral presents under the Christmas tree
which to open first, joy or woe?
Dwell on each one in turn

languish in romantic crushes
bathe in moments of ecstasy
shudder with the pain
sink in disappointment

life's intricate woven world of emotion
enveloped in a sea of memories

succumb to the erotic
dabble with the psychotic
emerge sanctified

privately smug in your personal desires
hidden from reality
living life like you love it

caress your thoughts
submit to their glory
all entwined
forever divine.

'Man was born to love
Though often he has sought
Like Icarus, to fly too high
And far too lonely than he ought
To kiss the sun of East and West
And hold the world at his behest
To hold the terrible power
To whom only gods are blessed
But me, I am just a man.'

Faith No More
Just A Man

I drew inspiration from Albert Camus, Alexander Solzhenitsyn, Anaïs Nin, Art Blakey, Bad Religion, Beastie Boys, Ben Harper, Big Black, Billie Holiday, Black Flag, Bob Marley, Bruce Springsteen, Charles Bukowski, Charlie Parker, CIV, Danny Sugerman, Dante, Dead Kennedys, Faith No More, Fugazi, Glen E. Friedman, Guru, Helmet, Henry Rollins, H20, Hunter S. Thomson, Ian Mackaye, Jean-Paul Sartre, John Coltrane, John Peel, Kenny Dalglish, Kurt Cobain, Michael Leunig, Miles Davis, Minor Threat, Nice 'N' Sleazy, Papillon, Peter Bagge's *Hate*, Primo Levi, Rancid, Sex Pistols, Shane MacGowan, Shelter, Social Distortion, Stiff Little Fingers, *Thrasher* magazine, The God Machine, The Fabulous Furry Freak Brothers, Tim Armstrong, Tool.

'Art is not a mirror to reflect the world but a hammer with which to shape it.'

Vladimir Mayakovsky